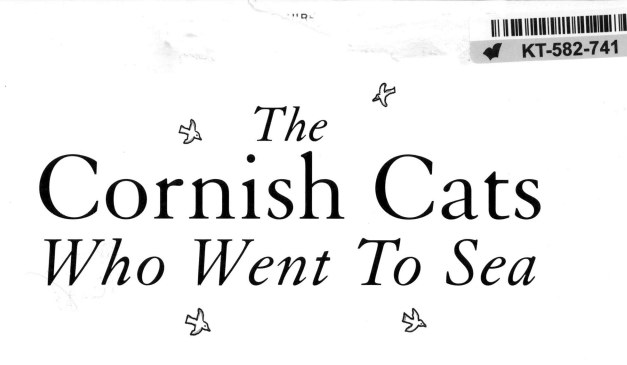

The
Cornish Cats
Who Went To Sea

Whiskers

Ginger Tiger

Fluffy

Mittens

Sam

To Theo

HAPPY CAT BOOKS

Published by Happy Cat Books Ltd.,
Bradfield, Essex CO11 2UT, UK

This edition first published 2004
3 5 7 9 10 8 6 4 2

Text and illustrations copyright © Michelle Cartlidge 1992, 2004

A CIP catalogue record for this book is available from the British Library

ISBN 1 903285 92 5

Printed in China

The Cornish Cats
Who Went To Sea

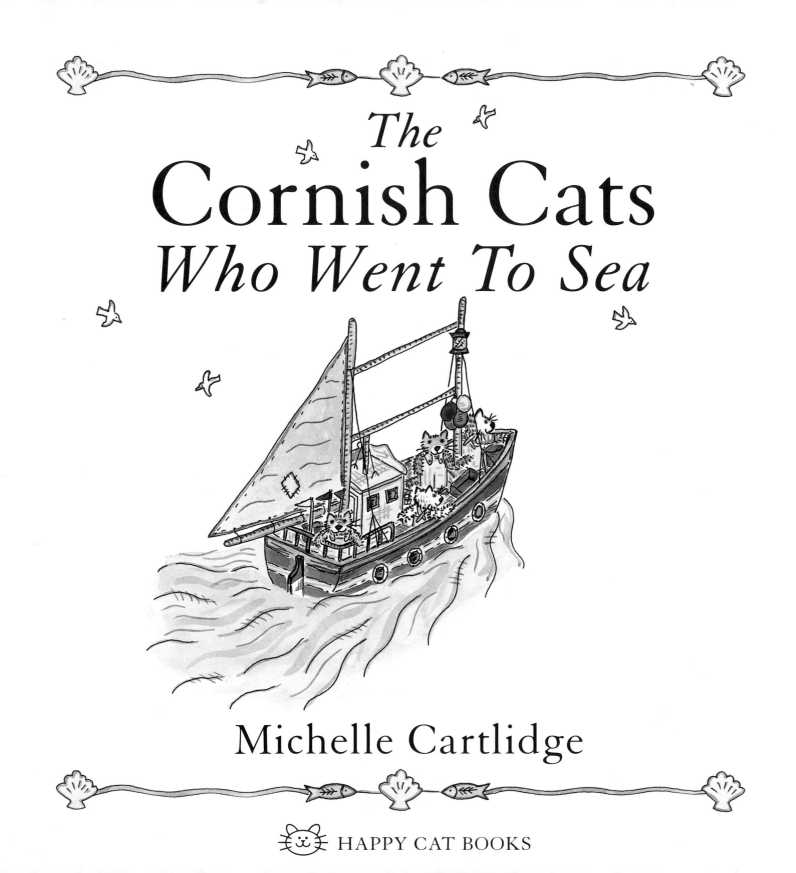

Michelle Cartlidge

HAPPY CAT BOOKS

Fluffy and her friends lived by a big, bustling fish market, in the harbour of a small fishing village.

Sitting on the harbour wall the cats watched the fishing boats leaving early in the morning and returning late at night, brimming with fresh fish.

Fluffy and her friends loved fish. They would stare at the slippery, gleaming catch and miaow hopefully. But all they got was, 'Shoo!' and 'Scat cat!' as the fishermen chased them away.

One night, as the cats prowled the empty fish market, Fluffy had an idea. Fluffy's ideas were famous. 'We'll go to sea, in a boat, and do some fishing ourselves.' And she told the other cats her plan.

'Fantastic!' miaowed all the cats in reply, 'that way we can catch all the fish we want to eat!'

The next day Ginger Tiger took them to his cousin's abandoned old boat. 'It's rather full of holes,' Whiskers said doubtfully.

Quickly the cats set to work and with hammers, nails and bits of old driftwood they mended the boat. Ginger Tiger painted the cabin bright yellow, Mittens swabbed the decks and Whiskers ran a flag up the mast.

Meanwhile Sam and
Fluffy searched the
village for useful things
for the journey. Sam
found a fishing net, some
food and a torch,

and Fluffy found a pair of
wellington boots and
managed to borrow a
compass and a telescope.

When they arrived back at the boat Ginger Tiger, Mittens and Whiskers were basking in the afternoon sun. The boat looked bright and shipshape. She was ready to sail.

'We leave at daybreak tomorrow,' said Fluffy, 'and nobody is to be late.'

The following day, at the crack of dawn, the cats were aboard ship and quietly edging out of the harbour towards the open sea.

Soon they could see the shoreline getting smaller and smaller, disappearing behind them.

All morning
they sailed

and all afternoon
they fished.

The nets were cast over and over again but not one fish was caught, just a few sprats which were barely enough to go round.

As night fell Mittens said, 'Oh dear, we don't seem to be very good at fishing.'

'Nonsense,' said Fluffy. 'Today was just a practice. Tomorrow we'll do better.'

To cheer them up Whiskers cooked a delicious fish soup with the sprats.

Sam played his guitar and together they sang songs.

Later, under the bright moonlight, they stayed up well into the night playing cards.

I n the morning they woke up early and took up their positions on the boat; their enthusiasm returned.

Just then Fluffy spotted a large shoal of fish a little way ahead of them. 'Quick, cast the nets, cats. We're in for a catch!' she shouted.

Soon they were hauling fish over the sides of the boat and into the buckets.

They had landed a spectacular catch; they had sole, plaice, mackerel, and even a few crabs. The boat was full.

'Hooray!' shouted the cats and they danced around the deck in celebration.

'Full steam ahead for home,' said Fluffy happily.

Suddenly the sky darkened. Lightning flashed, the rain beat down and the thunder boomed. It was a storm.

The cats howled. The violent rocking of the boat scared them. Their fur was drenched. 'Miaow! Miaow!'

The ship's wheel spun round wildly, the compass went haywire, and the boat tossed and turned on the waves.

There was only one thing left to do – Ginger Tiger knew he must call to the coastguard for help on the ship's radio.

'*Mayday, Mayday, Mayday,*' he called.

The coastguard was not pleased with the cats and told them that real sailors listen to the weather broadcasts. Earlier that morning there had been a gale warning.

The coastguard wasn't too angry though because the cats weren't all that far from port. He was able to tell them exactly how to steer their course home.

The storm began to subside and the cats could once again enjoy their journey, knowing they would soon be home.

As they sailed into the harbour the news of their fishing trip had spread and many other cats had gathered along the jetty to meet them, cheering and waving handkerchiefs. Fluffy and Ginger Tiger tied up the boat and laid out their catch on the quayside.

Soon there was a long queue of cats waiting, and the delicious fresh fish was quickly passed down the line.

They were five very happy fisher cats!

Whiskers

Ginger Tiger

Fluffy

Mittens

Sam